Great Disasters

by David Orme

Rans∞m

Trailblazers

Great Disasters
by David Orme
Educational consultant: Helen Bird

Illustrated by Martin Bolchover

Published by Ransom Publishing Ltd.
51 Southgate Street, Winchester, Hants. SO23 9EH
www.ransom.co.uk

ISBN   978 184167 694 4

First published in 2009

'Get the Facts' section - images copyright: earthquake 'concept' - Alex Slobodkin; apartment building (earthquake) - Robert van Beets; Lybian desert - Tobias Helbig; rat - Fabian Guignard; tsunami, Thailand - David Rydevik; flood, New Orleans after Katrina - NOAA; lightning, tornado - NOAA Photo Library, NOAA Central Library, OAR / ERL / National Severe Storms Laboratory (NSSL); hurricane - Donald Gruener; blizzard - Bill Grove; stormy sunset - Clint Spencer; earthquake devastation - William Walsh; Naples - Danilo Ascione; Krakatoa - flydime; candles - John Steele; RMS Titanic - NOAA; Chernobyl - International Nuclear Safety, http://insp.pnl.gov; hot springs - Yellowstone National Park Service; 9/11 - Lyle Owerko; Earth, comet - NASA/JPL.

Great Disasters

Contents

Get the facts   **5**

What is a disaster?   6

Natural disasters – the weather   8

Natural events – what the Earth can do   10

Man-made events – famous accidents   12

Man-made events – wars and terrorism   14

Mega-disasters past and future   16

Fiction

The Eruption   19

Great Disasters word check   **36**

Great Disasters

Get the facts

What is a disaster?

It is an event when hundreds
or even thousands of people die.

These are
natural disasters ...

Drought

Tsunami

Earthquake

Volcano

Flood

Is being ill a disaster?

IT IS, IF THOUSANDS OF PEOPLE DIE.

The Black Death came to Europe in the 1340s.

Most scientists think the disease was spread by **fleas** from **rats**.

Probably over 75 million people died.

In **1918** there was an outbreak of **flu**. **Fifty million people** may have died. It mainly affected young, healthy people.

It wasn't me!

Diseases like this may affect the world again.

Natural disasters – the weather

Weather often causes disasters.

Tornadoes only strike a small area, but the winds are so powerful the effects are very serious.

Hurricanes can cause huge damage.

Lightning injures around 2,000 people each year. Around 500 – 600 are killed.

Heavy rain or **snow** can cause damage and put lives at risk.

Bad weather can often cause floods. This table shows some of the worst ever floods.

When	Where	What happened	The effects
February 2000	Mozambique	Heavy rain and melting snow made the rivers burst their banks. A bad storm made things worse.	Two million people were affected. 25,000 were made homeless. About 800 were killed.
August 2005	Southern USA	Hurricane Katrina was the third strongest hurricane ever to hit the USA. It destroyed much of the city of New Orleans.	New Orleans was badly flooded because the hurricane had destroyed the city's flood defences.
1931	The Yellow River flood, China	The worst natural disaster ever?	As many as 4 million people may have died.

New Orleans after Hurricane Katrina.

Natural events – what the Earth can do

Earthquakes happen when energy stored in the Earth is released suddenly.

The ground shakes, buildings fall down and often great cracks open at the surface.

Volcanoes

The Italian volcano **Mount Vesuvius** erupted in the year 79 CE. The cities of **Pompeii** and **Herculaneum** were buried so completely that people forgot they were there for hundreds of years.

A woman killed when Mount Vesuvius erupted.

Mount Vesuvius and the ruins of Pompeii.

Vesuvius is still one of the most **dangerous volcanoes** in the world. Hundreds of thousands of people live close by. Will there be another eruption soon?

In 1883 a whole island exploded! The eruption of **Krakatoa** made the loudest noise ever reported. It was heard as far away as Australia (3,000 km away!).

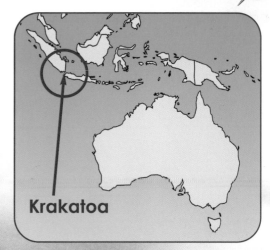

Krakatoa

The explosion set off **tsunamis** with waves over 30 metres high.

Thousands of people were killed or injured.

What is a tsunami?

A tsunami is a great wave. It can be caused by:

- An underwater earthquake.

- A great mass of rock falling into the sea.

The waves only become dangerous when they reach shallow water near the coast.

Man-made events – famous accidents

The Hillsborough disaster

April 1989

This happened because thousands of football fans crowded into the Hillsborough stadium in Sheffield, England.

An extra gate was opened. Football fans inside were crushed against fences as thousands more rushed in. 94 people died on the day and over 700 more were injured.

The Tay Bridge disaster

December 1879

This bridge in Scotland was badly made. When a violent storm shook the bridge, the middle part collapsed. A train fell into the icy river. More than 75 people died.

Before ... and after.

The sinking of the Titanic

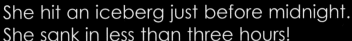

April 1912

RMS Titanic was the largest passenger ship in the world.

She set off on her maiden voyage in April 1912. Many rich and famous people were on board.

She hit an iceberg just before midnight. She sank in less than three hours!

There were not enough lifeboats for everyone, and 1,500 people died.

The wreck of the Titanic was discovered by Robert Ballard, in 1985.

The Hindenburg

During the 1920s and 1930s, people thought that airships were the best way to travel by air. But the gas they were filled with could catch fire easily.

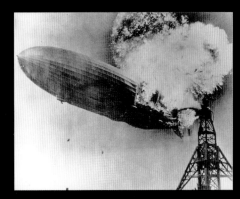

The Hindenburg was a huge German airship. In 1937 it flew to America. It burst into flames before the passengers could get off. 36 people died.

Man-made events – wars and terrorism

August 1945

The bombing of Hiroshima and Nagasaki

At the end of World War 2, **atomic bombs** were dropped on these Japanese cities.

Over 200,000 people died. Many more died later from the effects of **radiation**.

The Chernobyl disaster

April 1986

This was a major accident at a **nuclear power plant**. The area was contaminated by the **radioactive fallout**. Over 300,000 people had to be moved from their homes.

About 50 people died in the accident.

Many more died because of illness caused by the radiation.

Chernobyl – before, and after.

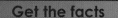
9/11

September 2001

On 11th September 2001, four planes were hijacked by **terrorists**. Two of them were flown into the twin towers of the **World Trade Center** in **New York**. The buildings collapsed. Nearly 3,000 people died.

75

Mega-disasters past and future

There have been really huge events in the past, bigger than anything you have read about so far.

These mega-disasters may happen again!

A **supervolcano** is an eruption which is thousands of times larger than normal.

In Yellowstone Park in the USA, the ground is rising.

It is a huge area. If it erupted it could cause total devastation.

A huge part of America would be impossible to live in. The climate of the world would be affected.

Pocket Basin, Yellowstone Park

A **comet** or **asteroid** may hit the Earth. This has happened in the past. The dinosaurs were probably all killed off when a very large meteorite hit.

In Siberia in 1908, **The Tunguska Event** flattened all the trees in an area over 2,000 square kilometres.

This was probably caused by an asteroid exploding just above the Earth's surface.

An **asteroid** will come close to the Earth in 2029.

Scientists believe it will not hit the Earth, but because it will come very close, the Earth's orbit may change!

17

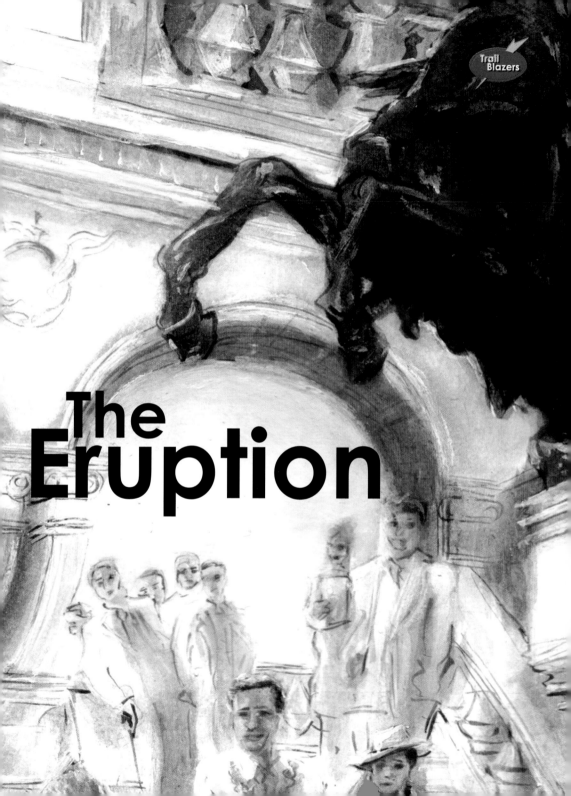

The Eruption

Chapter 1:
The volcano

You could see the volcano from anywhere in the city.

It had last erupted five hundred years ago. There were only villages around the volcano then. Lava had poured down the sides of the volcano, but everyone had escaped in time.

'The volcano is extinct now,' the experts said. 'Anyway, if it was going to erupt, there would be plenty of warning.'

There was no danger, the mayor said. Nothing to worry about.

But then the earthquakes began.

The first earthquakes were small, just enough to rattle the cups on the shelves. People asleep hardly noticed them.

Then one morning, just as people were setting off to work, there was a more powerful quake. Tiles fell from roofs. This time, the cups tumbled to the floor and smashed. One man was badly hurt as the quake shook him from a ladder.

'Don't worry,' said the Mayor. 'It's nothing to do with the volcano.'

But when people saw smoke and steam coming from the side of the volcano, they weren't so sure.

Chapter 2:
At the stables

In his cottage at the edge of the city, Gary Grimmer was worried. His riding school needed tourists. It was summer, and this was when he made most money. But the tourists had been scared away by the volcano.

Some of his friends were packing up and leaving.

'Get your family out now, Gary,' they said. 'The volcano is waking up.'

Gary's mum and dad lived in the cottage. They helped out with the riding school. Should he take them somewhere safe, just in case?

Early one morning, a few days later, there was another quake – a big one. The family heard the sound of smashing plates from the kitchen downstairs.

Gary banged on his parents' bedroom door.

'Mum, Dad! Look at the volcano!'

They rushed to the window.

A great column of smoke was hanging over the volcano. Already, grey ash was drifting down into the fields.

Chapter 3:
The horses won't move

'Let's get out of here – quick!' said Gary.

'What about the horses?' asked Martha, Gary's mum.

'We'll saddle them up and ride to Green Town,' said Gary. That will be much better than using the car. The roads will be crowded.'

The wind was blowing the ash away from Green Town. Gary was sure they would be safe there.

There were three horses at the stables. They saddled them up and rode out of the city.

Half way to Green Town, the horses stopped. Gary and his mum and dad tried to make them go forward, but they wouldn't move.

Chapter 4:
Eruption

'They want to turn around and head back to the city!' said Martha. 'What's wrong with them?'

'Maybe they know something we don't,' said Gary. 'Let's trust them.'

The horses set off back to the city at a gallop. When they got there the streets were empty, though the ash had stopped falling now.

Suddenly there was a roaring sound, and the ground shook.

'Look!' yelled Gary's dad. 'The volcano's blown!'

One side of the volcano had exploded. Black dust filled the sky, and a great cloud of scorching gas poured down, burning everything in its path.

The cloud missed the city, and within weeks everything was back to normal.

But Green Town was completely destroyed.

Great Disasters word check

airship

asteroid

black death

climate

comet

contaminated

devastation

earthquake

eruption

extinct

drought

hurricane

hydrogen

iceberg

lava

lifeboat

maiden voyage

meterorite

nuclear power plant

passenger

radiation

supervolcano

tornado

tourist

tsunami